SPEED OF LIGHT

STEFAN DURHAM

NEWMAN SPRINGS PUBLISHING
320 Broad Street
Red Bank, NJ 07701

First originally published by Newman Springs Publishing 2023

ISBN 979-8-88763-281-0 (Paperback)
ISBN 979-8-88763-282-7 (Digital)

Printed in the United States of America

In a realm where miracles are real and mystical powers exist, these are also both negative energy and positive energy. But when you conjure up ancient and powerful dark energies that you know nothing about, things can go absolutely wrong. It always will when you're living on a planet where sorcery and technology are one and the same, making it possible for one to manifest anything based on their level of awareness and how elevated their consciousness is.

This is an age before time became a construct of the mind, when people only kept track of their reality by means of cosmic and celestial bodies. However, this was an unknown age for which the world had been in perpetual darkness, ever since the original indigenous tribes were broken up and separated because of the thirst for power and control over who may be allowed to use their gifts and abilities.

Chaos and conflict became widespread throughout the entire proximity of this world; therefore, many wars followed these ideas and practices, which resulted in slavery. Now these slaves are what's left of the utopian societies that populated this region of the planet called Topez! This is where those who are still in power develop their technology by making slaves mine for precious resources such as gold, crystals, and other types of rare minerals.

Things like currency, science, and other technological devices all have their place in the modern world. But these modern conveniences at one point did not even matter when civilization in this realm first began, which means that there are ancient laws and principles encoded and inscribed in our DNA, to be passed down orally through expressive ceremonial practices.

These oral traditions eventually became what is now known as a written language. Some of these ancient stories and legends say that inside infinity, there are eight states of being and eight entities that exist inside of these dimensions.

These entities, called *Octagons*, are a group of biomechanical and cybernetic deities that have godlike abilities.

These entities are known for wearing a synthetic humanlike skin as a costume to blend in, which they refer to as *soft-wear*, in order to cover up their true identities, as well as to function properly in the material realm since their original forms are shapeless and are made up of pure consciousness.

Legends and myths suggest that the Octagons created and began the first civilization in this particular star system because of the abundance of powers and abilities they possess.

A prophecy was made that a young child would restore balance. When this child was found at the age of nine by the Octagons sent to destroy the child, on the ninth day of the thirteen lunar cycles, something spectacular and unexpected happened.

The Octagons attempted to combine their powers to destroy the child, but the child absorbed all eight of these powers and became *Kalli-Atune*, which in this realm means "the star seed," one chosen to be a conduit, a vessel that the ancient ancestors can inhabit and into which they could deposit messages in order to keep ancient and forgotten practices alive in the flesh.

This story takes place over two hundred thousand years ago when the planet Earth was still called Pangaea.

A wanderer and nomad by the name of Zenthaus is the last known member of his tribe, *Blue-rays*, who are the descendants of powerful cosmic beings from Pluto. The *Plutonians* give honor and reverence to the stingray as their deity and queen mother goddess. Because of the sacred markings on their bodies, they are known to summon and activate star gates, which are doorways or portals into other realms and dimensions.

One morning, when Zenthaus was resting at the mouth of a cave in a remote area where he occupies several of the cave systems, he was awakened by a crying voice, a woman's voice! "Please, please, help my child!" said the voice.

Rushing off the ground, standing up so quickly just to see there was no one around, made him think that he must have been dreaming. Instead of going back to sleep, he had a strong urge to meditate.

Usually, he would choose to meditate inside the cave where it was more peaceful and isolated. For some reason, he decided to go to a nearby hilltop.

Ten minutes into his meditation, he was startled by the voice again, and this time the voice was undeniably loud and clear. This time he could tell that this voice was coming from the northwest area across the desert where the Dragon Court operates.

Slaves were not allowed to bear children unless permitted by the Dragon Court council, so most children were raised in secret or discarded into the nearby desert where anything barely survived. This was a normal practice for the Dragon Court. They were so notorious and ruthless that their mercy would still be considered an act of cruelty.

Immediately, Zenthaus called on Kano, who at the time was his only friend and companion, a mammoth-sized white wolf. Such were extremely rare and majestic creatures that came from the mountain and forest regions of Pangaea.

Zenthaus never really left the area he lived in unless absolutely necessary, but he was compelled to follow the voice and make sure that it was even real. He was determined to help heal the planet and bring it back from unfavorable conditions, to restore sacred knowledge to a lost and forgotten civilization.

As they began in the direction where he believed the voice was coming from, again he heard the woman's voice so clearly in his head that it was almost as if she was communicating with him telepathically!

So they quickly ride off into the desert where it took a *Markaba Hermonica* to cross. This was an ancient practice and tradition represented by three days, meaning that the people in this part of the world would use time periods to measure large distances.

Zenthaus thought to himself that in order to cover a distance of this size, he would need to try and complete the journey in half the time. There was a strong sense of urgency attached to the voice he heard. At this time it was already midday, so he figured that traveling by night would be the best way, especially because this particular desert was full of nearly extinct prehistoric creatures of all kinds. During the daytime, there were countless pterodactyl birdlike reptiles that would occupy the sky over this part of the desert. The struggle for survival in this area would be extremely difficult for most.

Certain myths and legends mention how Pangaea used to be a much greener and more fertile tropical planet, abundant with life and culture. Because of ongoing wars on the surface, as well as cosmic wars above, the planet was brought highly advanced knowledge and weapons from other worlds and star systems, ending in the destruction of much of the surface of the planet. This caused vitrification, a chemical process that turns solid rock into glass, and this resulted in the making of many wastelands and deserts.

After these tragedies wiped out more than half of Pangaea's preexisting populations, along with most of the plant life and animal species, this highly advanced knowledge became forbidden and forgotten.

This challenge did not hold Zenthaus back.

Perhaps for reasons that are unknown, or it might be because he was the last of his kind and had nothing else to lose, his determination and bravery allowed him to override any fears or doubts that he may have felt in that moment.

Trying their best to be discreet, they swiftly hurried into the desert, running cautiously without letup.

The next morning, they started to slow down since they had been running all night. They needed to seek out some sort of shelter or a place for rest mainly because it gets extremely hot in the morning and scorching by midday.

They stopped to take a drink of water when suddenly, Zenthaus noticed a nearby opening in the ground, so they went to investigate. As they got closer to the opening, Kano fearlessly went in ahead of him. Zenthaus quickly followed into the dark large sandy opening.

When they got inside, the sand poured down like a waterfall. As their eyes adjusted to the dense darkness, and with the only sunlight now being blocked by pouring sand, they realized that they were surrounded by a network of tunnels. After resting for a while, they carefully chose a tunnel and began to walk.

As they faced the darkness, their only light source came from a wooden staff that Zenthaus carried, with a black tourmaline crystal attached to the end that can illuminate on command. After walking for hours, they saw another opening.

Here was where they discovered an unbelievably large underground pyramid-like structure.

As they moved closer, right away he recognized markings on what seemed to be ancient ruins. There was no trace of any life or activity. Shockingly, Zenthaus realized that these symbols belong to what was only thought to be a myth. These were the signs and symbols of a technologically advanced race of humanoid hybrids that were half human and half scorpion called *Scorpionics*!

These beings carried highly advanced weapons shaped like spears that shoot out an ectoplasmic substance, disintegrating whatever it comes in contact with.

Zenthaus only heard stories of them but had never before seen one of their kind in person.

Backing away slowly, he signaled to Kano to come over, but for some reason, Kano eagerly ran into one of the entrances as if he was chasing something. Although he knew how risky it would be, Zenthaus quickly followed Kano without hesitating, into this ancient and mysterious triangular structure. Inside it was extremely dark and difficult to see. Using the light from his crystal, he was able to see at least ninety-three degrees around him and up to nine feet in front of him. It seemed to be noticeably larger inside than it was outside. Judging by the massive column statues, it was almost like this section of the construction they were in must have been thousands of square feet.

"Kano, wait, come back," Zenthaus said, running as fast as he can to catch up. He notices a brilliant bright light. A room lit up, glowing and flashing a greenish color at the end of a long narrow hallway. Zenthaus figured that Kano was somehow drawn to the light or the low vibrational frequency and sound coming from it. When entering the room, right away he noticed a bright green orb hovering above what looked like a pool of mercury, which must have been the source of their technology. Not wanting to be seen, they both quickly leave the room, going back the other direction, heading for the exit.

Just as soon as they get outside of the pyramid, before Zenthaus even realizes anything, he gets struck in the face with an object.

As he regains his focus, immediately he realizes that the object was none other than a six-foot scorpion tail. This was no ordinary scorpion tail because this one was more mechanical and robotic in nature, which was a lot different than what he was told about the description of this species. He took it literally instead of symbolically.

One by one, more Scorpionics began to appear and reveal themselves in a synchronized order, almost as if they were instructed to do so, from some sort of cloaking device.

Instinctively, Kano lashed out at one of the Scorpionics, grabbing hold of one of their metallic spears and snapping it like a twig in his mouth. At that point, they were completely surrounded, and there must have been at least a dozen or more Scorpionic soldiers that they could see, speaking in a rare, outdated and yet still understandable language.

One of them spoke and said, "You are trespassing on sacred and forbidden ground, so now our queen will decide your consequences."

With all their weapons pointed at Zenthaus and Kano, the soldiers made them walk back into the pyramid, this time in another direction connected to a different section or chamber, the queen's chamber.

Once they entered, it was nothing like Zenthaus expected. Inside the queen's chamber was a virtual reality, a visually spectacular simulation and display of the planetary system that they and their ancestors originated from, which was somewhere in the Orion star system. It was astonishing!

As they approached the queen, Zenthaus noticed how young and beautiful she was. She was covered and draped in many different materials precious metals, gemstones, and brilliant colors.

"How did you find this place?" she said, and with a tremendous amount of authority. She asked again, "Why have you come here?"

"I mean no harm or disrespect. We are just passing through!" Zenthaus replied.

The queen responded, "No one has ever seen this place and lived, for we have been living in secret for hundreds of years!"

Impressed by the size and magnificence of Kano, the queen offers Zenthaus an alternative that if he leaves Kano behind, he would then gain the right to pass.

Zenthaus could not bear the thought of leaving Kano, especially because he raised Kano from a wolf pup.

He thought that if he didn't comply, then all their efforts might be for nothing and he would die anyway, so he took a second to think.

Zenthaus replied, "No! I cannot and will not leave my only friend here. And for that, I am not sorry."

Shocked by what she heard, for a few moments this divinely powerful queen was caught off guard by the way Zenthaus remained so calm and expressionless, almost as if he did not even fear the consequences.

Zenthaus never once thought of himself as Kano's master. They had always lived as equals. Besides that, Zenthaus was a master of himself, which meant having complete balance and control over one's self, both emotionally and energetically. Zenthaus knew to abstain from violent actions in order to keep them both alive, long enough to later escape. This made the situation more mysterious because it was extremely difficult to read his vibration.

By order of the queen, they were both taken separately to different remote locations within the structure, going deeper into different dimensions underground where they were about to witness the most astonishing, exquisite limestone formations ever seen before.

Without much water, one might not expect to find any signs of life this far down, but beneath the dry and scorched desert landscape lay a subterranean wonderland. Full of life underground, freshwater and saltwater river currents were where its secrets remained hidden and unknown until now.

The walls were covered with the most fragile and delicate of crystals. Many of these crystals were made of gypsum, a mineral that comes from limestone.

As they went deeper into the structure, it connected to an underground cave system below, where there were whole galleries filled with the most unusual formations, like five-meter cones frosted with the shiniest crystals.

There is, in fact, more life here than anyone would think possible, despite the pools of sulfuric acid and low levels of oxygen.

The biggest surprise is something altogether more bizarre.

Because of their ability to survive in such extreme conditions, this colony of creatures was able to thrive in a world without sunlight. They would extract energy from the hydrogen sulfide gas, the basis of a food chain, which among other creatures supports a remarkable ecosystem.

It seemed as if this subterranean species understood the importance of self-preservation, which makes sense how this ancient culture has managed to remain in secret for so long.

After being taken to a small room, Zenthaus began to meditate. During his meditation, he was given a sign where he was visited by three of his ancestors, who when contacted are described as angelic in nature, not just from their appearance as "light figures" or "bodies of light," but also because of the knowledge that they impart.

Zenthaus was able to receive specific instructions and reminders about the mission he set out on and the importance of it, realizing that it is a part of his destiny and life purpose.

In their message, they helped him understand that the completion of this mission will determine if he would be exalted to a higher position and be able to exist in much higher realms like the ascended masters before him or get recycled back into the planet's digestive tract. They went on to explain that when we look at the comparisons to the way the planet functions, there are similarities to the way the human body functions as well. So when it comes to ascension, we can think of that process as the planet's way of releasing you back into the cosmos in your original gaseous form or ethereal body, like a person breathing in fresh air and then exhaling and releasing us back out like the carbon-based beings that we are.

According to their teachings, anything that is created from this unified state of existence is infused with the will to return or be resurrected back into oneness to start the cycle all over again, wiser than before because of the experience that has been simulated.

While still meditating, he was also told that he had always been selected to fulfill this particular assignment regarding the woman's voice he heard, and that her child is the chosen star seed who is supposed to restore balance but is now in danger of being discovered and discarded.

At this point, Zenthaus was granted access to activate a brand-new, special, rare ability to complete his mission. He was now allowed to manifest a rift in space that creates a doorway into any specific location that he can imagine, with enough focus and concentration. Before, he could only manifest certain portals at specific times of the month when the moon can be seen during the day. Now although able to travel interdimensionally through time and space where various entities dwell, he would still not know the extent of his new abilities for years to come.

After awakening from his deep, meditative state, Zenthaus was invigorated with confidence and then able to understand more fully about what motivated him. After practicing a number of times, he was able to create a large enough opening to walk through. The only problem was that he could only create doorways into places where he had already been before or that carried his energy signature, which meant that he would have to first find out where they took Kano. It presented a challenge in such a tremendously broad and spacious dwelling place.

The first thing he needed was to retrieve the staff that was taken from him by the Scorpionic soldier who struck him in the face, almost knocking him out! He also happened to be standing guard right outside the space Zenthaus was being kept in.

Just by touching the wall, with certain intentions, he was able to almost immediately transform the entire wall into what resembled a metallic liquid with a watery fabric texture that he was able to clearly see through. Now, he could see the soldier and his wooden staff.

Catching the soldier off guard, he jumped through, quickly snatching the staff as he knocked the soldier out simultaneously.

While deep in thought, he then realized that he was in an unknown area and there were just too many rooms to search through, but with his newfound purpose, Zenthaus was unbothered by these circumstances. Clearly, the information he received during meditation gave him a sense of inner calmness and understanding. Knowing that he was being guided by very powerful cosmic beings and feeling like his abilities were somehow enhanced helped his state of mind as well.

While closing his eyes and taking a deep breath, he was able to see in his mind's eye exactly where Kano had been kept. Zenthaus manifested a mirrorlike portal through which he was able to walk. He now entered the space where Kano was being held along with many other caged animals and creatures that he could not readily identify. It appeared like some were being experimented on. Some were freakishly and disproportionately larger than normal.

Suddenly, a soldier noticed Zenthaus in the cage next to Kano and called out to the others. The soldiers quickly filled the room, pointing their weapons.

Zenthaus attempted to manifest a large enough doorway for him and Kano to walk through. For some reason, he was unable to do so; it was not working. It appeared that the cage they were in was made of some kind of unique and unknown metal, a transparent aluminum alloy that somehow was able to block his abilities.

While it was seeming like there was nothing more that could be done, they both stood there watching as the Scorpionic soldiers moved in on them.

As soon as the cage got opened, Kano lunged at the soldiers in an attempt to protect his friend. At the same time, Zenthaus yelled out, "No!" By then, it was already too late. Kano sacrificed himself for Zenthaus to get away to safety.

As Kano fought with over a dozen soldiers, they began forming a circle to surround him. Without hesitating, they shot their powerful energy-based weapons all at once, vaporizing and killing him instantly.

Zenthaus had to watch his only friend be taken away from him in one instant, one moment.

With precision and synchronization, they all aimed their weapons back at Zenthaus. By then he was already outside of the cage, and just by thinking about it, he quickly conjured up another portal entry that would lead him right back to where he first discovered the opening on the desert surface.

One of the soldiers followed Zenthaus through the gateway between time and space, where they both met face to face on the other side.

This particular soldier wanted payback for being caught off guard and knocked out; Scorpionic soldiers were skilled warrior-assassins, combative by nature.

When things couldn't get any worse, as they began to fight to the death, they noticed a sandstorm in the distance heading in their direction. The sandstorm was approximately six kilometers away, moving at twenty-five miles per hour. There was only a short distance between the two of them and the storm for him to battle with the soldier in enough time and to teleport without being followed. With their lives now hanging in the balance, they fought tirelessly.

Meanwhile, Zenthaus thought about Kano and how they always lived by a specific code. This was one of the only things that Zenthaus can remember about his people, as they would say, "Sonjaro Rukutu," which means, "Live good. Die great." And today, like most days, he was ready for that outcome, because his people and their ancestors viewed death much differently than most cultures.

Kano most definitely died in a great way, sacrificing himself for someone else. This gave Zenthaus the inspiration and activation he needed to complete his mission, knowing that Kano's death would mean much more if he himself continued on.

The sandstorm drew near, yet the two of them did not back down or show any signs of fearfulness.

Just when it seemed like they were both about to be consumed by the oncoming storm, the Scorpionic soldier jumped up and dove directly into the sand like a pool of water and disappeared.

Zenthaus hurries up to open a doorway. Facing the storm, he opens one and walks into it, looking as though he walked right into the storm.

Arriving near his destination, Zenthaus was now close enough to see where the Dragon Court Society was found. This was the closest he'd ever been to this location.

The Dragon Court, the only world power during this period, was an order made up of three basic yet organized levels whose council members were in charge of the "workers," who were the soldiers. The soldiers also had their own chain of command and were in control of the slaves.

Dragon Court members were known to be a part of an ancient race who were related to dragons, a reptilian species that were said to be the wisest of all the ancient cultures.

The outer gates of this enormous complex, which some would say was a power plant, revealed another wall, noticeably taller, circling all the way around and spiraling up to the entrance.

It was built on a mound of dirt that was handmade, so there was no easy way in or out of what looked like an extremely well-protected fortress.

The top was layered with gigantic blocks of marble put in place to serve as a landing strip for their airships that were also referred to by the slaves as flying shields because of their shape.

Please give me a sign. I need a sign, Zenthaus said to himself, hoping that he might get a visual of the woman, since he hadn't heard her voice since before he received confirmation through his meditation.

There didn't seem to be anyone around at first, so he proceeded, still saying to himself, *Here I am. Please. Say something. Let me see you.*

Before he could take another step, a creature of great size unexpectedly appeared out of nowhere, using some kind of camouflage. This was no ordinary creature. This was an Organite. These monstrosities were bred to guard this area where the Dragon Court ran their experiments.

Some may have heard of evolution, but these scientific experiments gave rise to a practice and phenomenon called "devolution," where creatures evolve in unnatural ways and have been genetically spliced for experimental purposes.

These inorganic beings had been reverse engineered and genetically modified to be something contrary to nature, so that on a conscious level, they evolve only backward, activating the portion of their brain that is responsible for aggression and violence.

With killer instinct, the Organite charged straight at Zenthaus. Still standing in place, he allowed the Organite to come closer and closer. When the creature came close enough, he folded space like a blanket, creating a window right away so fast that the Organite dove directly into the portal, sending it to an unknown part of the desert.

When looking up, Zenthaus saw that the wall behind the gate was really a frequency fence designed to block out interferences. A firewall! And for that moment, it was offline.

At this point, the opportunity presented itself for him to enter, so he went for it. At the same time, more Organites started to appear out of thin air. By then, Zenthaus was already on the other side of the outer gates where the bars were spaced apart just enough for him to fit through, but the Organites where just too massive to follow, for they were only made to guard the outside premises.

For the first time, he didn't have to wonder what it would look like once inside.

It was nothing like anything he could have ever expected. It was like he stepped into another dimension. To his surprise, he found himself standing in what resembled an indoor city, a technologically advanced metropolis with multiple species and complex varieties of exotic plant life, filled and populated by a slave class, a workforce! With a functioning economy where they manufactured parts for their airships and gathered natural elements such as rare minerals, crystals, herbs, and spices, this created an inner planetary market for other breakaway civilizations who come here form other worlds to visit.

As he stood there in shock and amazement, he began to realize that these people seemed to be unbothered by their captivity, almost like they were unaware of their slavery. Most of them were prisoners of war. Trying his best to act natural and blend in, Zenthaus removed the hood from his head, exposing his twisted locks! Not a common hairstyle for that particular era—a lot different than the style of braiding done by slaves.

These were different classes of slaves, and these particular slaves had unrestricted access to certain privileges, yet they were mentally imprisoned by the authority placed upon them.

Walking among them, Zenthaus caught the attention of a much older man.

"Who are you, stranger?" he yelled out, recognizing that this hairstyle belonged only to highly skilled mercenaries who were a part of the Blue-ray tribe. It appeared that the elderly slave could remember a time when this hairstyle was considered to be something dreadful, so Blue-rays were the most respected and most feared among all the ancient tribes; therefore, people would be in dread of their locks and what they identified them as.

Everyone backed away slowly from Zenthaus, except for one person, a young woman standing there as she looked unafraid. They approached one another.

"You look exactly the way you did in my dream," she said. "And I prayed that you would come to me."

How soft her voice is, he thought. The way she sounded was enchanting, and the way she pronounced her words was almost hypnotic and alluring. He responded, "Your request was made known to me, and how refreshing it is to hear your voice again. I came as soon as I could. Are you no longer in danger?"

"No, yet I am still afraid that you might be too late!" She went on to explain that her daughter, Allele, who is only nine years old, was just taken from her to be disposed of. Allele's father, who was a member of the Dragon Court, had already been put to death that same morning. She also said that they came from a rare bloodline on Xylanthea, a planet found near the Orion star system, populated by a royal family with psychic abilities.

These abilities allow this family to be telepathically linked together. This made the child both important and special.

"I can still feel her energy. You can save her if you go now," she said. "The older man is my grandfather, and I must stay with him and care for him."

Zenthaus said, "I will come back for you. What is your name? I am Zenthaus."

She responded, "Mazaya."

Making his way through the city, he began to realize that this place, although very high-tech and even pleasing to the eyes with trees and parklike areas, was no more than a holographic simulation!

This false reality enabled slaves to move about without shackles, making them believe that they still had a measure of freedom. *Fascinating*, he thought.

In actuality, they were suffering from a different form of slavery—mental slavery!

The reproductive and birth rate of slaves were controlled by means of chemical castration, where each were given a psychoactive substance, a composition directed through the food and water that induced submission and cooperation.

Zenthaus was trying to figure out where to go next when Mazaya spoke again inside of his head. It seemed that when they came into contact for the first time, there was an immediate exchange of energy between them, which now allowed them to both be telepathically joined together more indefinitely.

She let him know that Allele could be found in Foulmoor, an area located just outside of their base of operation where many children who were illegally born in secret and slaves who were no longer useful were abandoned.

Whenever there was chaos on any given planet throughout the cosmos, the universe always provided a solution in every generation to restore balance. The Dragon Court Society would do anything to prevent this balance from taking place in order to maintain power.

Foulmoor had very harsh, hostile, and unforgiving surroundings where there was barely any human life, only unknown numbers of reptilian birds and a variety of arachnid species. A field of debris, smoldering fire pits, and smoke columns blocked out the sunlight, making it seem like it was always proceeding to dusk. There were countless bone fragments that could be seen for miles. Sometimes mutants that no longer served a purpose or never fully developed were placed here and, for as long as they could. To survive, they fed on whatever could be found, making this place a living graveyard! And there was no sign of Allele.

In a state of despondency, he looked over, and there she was by herself, holding a large femur to protect herself. Zenthaus was relieved to see her still alive, but when he approached her, she backed away slowly. She was terrified!

"I was sent to you by your mother. Let me help you," he humbly said, with his hands raised. "My name is Zenthaus."

Before she could respond, they were distracted by the sound of thunder and the sight of plasma discharging from the ground and the sky. That sound was made by the Octagons, who transferred themselves from the southern quadrant of the galaxy at such great speed that it created an electromagnetic storm just above where Zenthaus and Allele were standing. Possibly these malevolent beings had knowledge of prophecy; therefore, they knew to be in this area at this exact moment. Otherwise they may have been simply alerted by the Dragon Court council members who had their own agenda and arrangements harvesting genetic material for generations.

Whether it was about prophecy or not, it became clear that they did not want the child to live.

Only two meters apart, they both tried to run toward each other. Willing to die himself, Zenthaus hoped that he might somehow shield or conceal her from the danger, but with laser-sharp precision each of the Octagons focus all their light photon energy, shooting it from their hands at Allele. Instead of killing her instantly, something else took place that day.

Having reached a certain age along with having a rare and unique blood type made Allele nearly indestructible at this point, which meant that the premonition Mazaya had about it being too late for Allele was really more about it being too late for the Dragon Court Society and the Octagons, now knowing the fulfillment of Allele's immortality. Yet she was still in need of Zenthaus and his ability to help her avoid captivity. What was intended that day was indeed the opposite. The light photons that would normally be harmful triggered a chemical reaction that allowed Allele to now absorb another's powers, each time making her stronger and more powerful.

Confused by something that had never happened before in history actually happening, Zenthaus grabbed Allele by the hand in an attempt to quickly escape.

They found themselves encapsulated within Allele's energetic biosphere, coming from the center of her chest, creating a 360-degree dome-like structure all around them. The electrical currents within the force field generated enough power to upgrade Zenthaus and increase his ability to fold space and manifest portals, transporting them instantaneously to the dark side of the moon.

These powers combining resulted in the DNA of the star seed altering, causing these numeric and genetic sequences to amplify Allele's gifts and abilities.

The synchronicities that took place on that day were activation codes that gave one access to specific, rare, and unique genetic powers and capabilities.

He wondered how this could be possible, since he had never personally been on the moon nor has any point of reference to remember. His ancient ancestors from Pluto would use this moon as an outpost alongside of another breakaway civilization on their way to help seed and populate Pangaea in the ancient past. These memories were stored in his DNA, giving Zenthaus the rare opportunity to travel somewhere he had never been before.

It turned out that the far side of the moon is really an abandoned seed colony.

Zenthaus would soon discover he has whole libraries of ancient knowledge and wisdom stored in his genetic memory bank. After many lifetimes, it continued to call out to bring forth new light and information.

*****

Allele

Growing up on the moon would at times seem strange. Seeing Pangaea from this distance sometimes would pique my curiosity. My teacher, Zenthaus, called it the teardrop due to the fact that Pangaea is a water-based planet and is made up of over 70 percent of salt water. He would use this metaphor as a teaching tool so that I could learn about my home planet and where I originally came from.

One day I asked him, *Was it a happy tear or a sad one?* He replied by saying, "Whether it may be tears of joy or sadness will depend on if your vibration is strong enough upon arrival, when we return. You are the chosen one who will help restore balance and prosperity."

At the time I didn't know what that meant, but he told me that it would make sense one day.

I learned deep metaphysical and esoteric knowledge about universal laws and principles on an astronomical level, which expanded my consciousness and awareness. He tells me that these teachings are forbidden and forgotten but, as the chosen star seed, I must learn this sacred wisdom so that someday I would be able to restore this balance in the world, bringing back the golden age, the Age of Light, where there is no more knowledge to be kept secret.

Zenthaus did not know my family and knew very little about where I came from. I haven't seen my mother's face in three years. Sometimes I can hear her voice clear as day, especially when I'm asleep or dreaming.

He would mention at different times that he promises to reunite us one day. For some reason I believe him.

He speaks a lot about how important and unique I am and, when I learn how to use my gifts properly, I would have unlimited potential. I'm still learning about what kind of abilities I possess and more importantly how to control them. All I know at this time is that my hands and feet glow and vibrate during meditation. Even randomly when I'm deep in thought or daydreaming. Whatever I think about in those moments would literally come into existence. It was an inconvenience that I would fly and teleport sometimes when I sleep, only to realize upon awakening that I'm in a different place than where I was when I lay down.

Zenthaus tells me that if I focus my intentions and concentrate, I can and will control my powers more fully but that these things take time and practice. For now, the extent of my capabilities are learning how to move objects with powers of perception, thoughts, and commanding the natural elements around me to become hot or cold; to change between solids, liquids, and gases.

*****

The fulfillment of the prophecy caused Allele to undergo many changes, magnifying the way that she processed light code frequencies. Her blood was becoming liquid crystal. Her cells and amino acid structures were replicating at a rate faster than before, causing her to go from iron- to copper-based blood cells, turning her skin green.

*****

Allele

Thanks to Zenthaus and his ability to be a great teacher, we were able to successfully terraform and recreate a more habitable and beautiful living space for us to train and practice undisturbed. For as long as we have, working together in making this part of the moon accommodating enough has kept my mind busy, but sometimes I wonder about who my father was.

We tried to make it as similar to our home as we possibly could, not as it is now, but in the ancient past; so it resembled a parklike oasis rich with plant life and water. Therefore, we had plenty of sustenance.

This side of the moon was always dark and cold like night, and we needed a source of light, so we also created beams or pillars of light that towered out of the ground all throughout the small secluded area we lived in. It also gave us polarized light—light that is reflected by water—creating its very own light source.

*****

One day during her meditation practice, Allele could not focus and also broke the concentration of her teacher by asking, "Are you my father?"

"No, I am not," Zenthaus replied.

"Where did I come from? And how was I made?"

It took a few moments to think about. The first question was simple, but the second one, a little more complicated.

After trying his best to formulate an illustration, he was able to best convey the differences between both masculine and feminine energies and that the two genders are both biological machineries. He described how the feminine body is organic, like technology similar to activating a star gate, which is a doorway to other realms and dimensions; the masculine harnesses massive amounts of energy, and with enough power generated—the power of love—a life form can be introduced into this physical plane of existence. "This is how we are all brought into this material realm," he imparted.

Even as a great master teacher, Zenthaus was not quite prepared for that specific teaching moment, but this allowed him to learn something about himself. Never before has he been more careful.

There were many parables that Zenthaus would use to teach about the physical body, environmental bodies, celestial bodies, and how everything in the universe is connected.

*****

Allele

As I gaze into the perfect blackness of deep space, into the vast and continuous expansion of the unknown, I wonder what else is possible. The unknown and unlimited amount of resources around us should make one feel rich. It is our birthright. That reality can only belong to those with an inner sense of knowing what is unknown to others, that there is no separation between the creators and the creation. We are all connected to Mother Earth, Father Sky, and the Sun and his moon goddess.

Today we leave this place for good and journey back home to Pangaea—which, after three and a half years, should only take about a billionth of a second, like walking through a door. Yet all I can think about is my mother and if she is still alive.

We made a bridge to get home by tapping into the moon's magnetism, pulling on its energy from the northern and southern hemisphere, creating a vortex forty feet wide in diameter. In a flash of light, we departed, leaving behind the markings of geometric shapes and patterns in the permafrost.

*****

Back on Pangaea, the chaos, confusion, and conflict grew tremendously, appearing as though Allele's absence lowered the vibration of the whole planet as never before; so proximity is key in the fulfillment of this journey.

Mazaya still grieved over the loss of Allele and her father. Although slightly weak at the moment due to the low vibratory state she had been left in since her daughter's disappearance, her abilities still allowed her to feel Allele's energy, giving her the reassurance that her daughter was still alive and well.

Without knowing exactly where Allele had gone, Mazaya had a strange correlation with the moon for some reason and was somehow intensely drawn to it. Without fail, every night she would look up at the moon and talk to it as if it were her daughter. Little did she know Allele had the very same practice, which meant that every night, as though through a mirror, they were staring back at each other.

Zenthaus felt that it was his responsibility to protect the star seed and reunite her with her mother. Now that he had found himself walking in his divine purpose, he wanted to free as many as he possibly could. Initially his plan was to free Mazaya and her grandfather, but now with Allele's help, they had a better chance of overthrowing the cursed ground that this operation rests upon. When the star seed reaches maturity, she would set even more minds free since there were multiple Dragon Court locations throughout this entire region. Her being initiated in the art of mastering the elements suggested that the odds were in their favor.

Stepping out of the vortex, their feet touched down on Pangaea's shimmering golden desert sand. Immediately, they were met with the Octagons along with the entire army of Dragon Court soldiers. They were still interested in running experiments on the star seed in order to learn the extent of her powers. The whole time they were eagerly anticipating, waiting, and planning for the arrival of the chosen star seed.

Caught off guard by the ambush, Zenthaus was unable to summon a portal fast enough to travel through again, and they were surrounded by an ocean of angry Dragon Court soldiers.

Quickly tearing the two of them apart like a fine silk cloth, they nearly beat Zenthaus to death, handing him over to the Dragon Court members. He would be put to death or registered as a slave. Whatever they decided, they would make sure that they were always the beneficiaries.

Allele saw what they did to her teacher, her father figure. She never exactly knew her real father and was raised in secret. She wasn't quite ready for a battle of this magnitude, especially without the help of Zenthaus. Consequently, out of pure, intense emotional rage, Allele's whole body burst into blue flames, shooting out light and molecules, causing half of the soldiers around her to become frozen stiff. They would go from a solid, to liquid, to a gas state as they evaporate in the face of the burning hot desert sun. Her efforts were not enough in that moment. She was taken with Zenthaus back to the base.

Am I dead? I must be dead, he thought. *But if I am dead, how is it that I am still conscious and aware? Is this what it is like?* Zenthaus wondered with amazement. A watery pool of comfort, encased in darkness, feeling no pain as though he had gone back into his mother's womb. When he opened his eyes, he found himself immersed inside a regeneration pod. All his broken bones and bruises were fully repaired by a special kind of liquid that corresponds with amniotic fluid, similar to what infants experience in utero.

No, he was not dead. In fact, he was still very much alive and, as the last known member of his tribe, they figured that they would gain more by keeping him in a state of existence, but as a slave.

Once released from the pod, he was picked up by two guards and was taken into the main lodge, where he was to be judged by Dragon Court officials as to what class of slave he would be and what level he would work on.

When he entered the room, it was circular, and each council member sat in their own space around the circle. There was no ceiling. The whole sky could be seen, like one could in an observatory.

"This one looks strong. Why not make him a soldier?" suggested one of the council members.

When Zenthaus looked up, he could not believe what he saw. Either he was hallucinating or it was some kind of trickery because to his surprise, it was what looked like his best friend, Kano, standing right next to the council member. But wait, this was not exactly the Kano he remembered. It was obvious that this wolf was gray, so they must have collected a hair sample at some point after Kano's capture. Although identical, this was no more than a clone, a reproduction of the original. It seemed that the Dragon Court were also in trade with the Scorpionics to harvest and manipulate genetic material.

On his way to be processed and be given a chemical lobotomy by needle injection, he could hear Mazaya's voice, just like a whisper in his head, say, "Please tell me you and Allele are okay, because I fear the worst."

Now that he was close enough, just like picking up a signal, their telepathic connection came back online.

"I am so sorry. I lost her again," he responded, with a slight quiver in his voice. "But I will find a way to bring her back to you. I give you my word." He understood the importance of their binding engagement and that they had an agreement.

Zenthaus planned to keep his word because he felt that he once again had something and someone to live for.

Mazaya said, "I believe you, but I really need that to be true right now because I lost my grandfather and I've been alone for almost two years. You and Allele are all the family I have now."

Zenthaus was able to hold that conversation in his head while still walking with the guards on his way to be stung—not by a Scorpion, and maybe it was with the Scorpionics that he should have taken his chances.

As soon as he received that very much needed confirmation from Mazaya, he knew how to act. Learning from his last encounter with the Organite, rather than just jumping through a portal himself, Zenthaus was going to make them jump instead. This time, he made the wall open up on command and pushed the two guards in.

Just moments before Allele was going to have her memory wiped clean, Zenthaus showed up in the room.

Here was where they created the chemical compositions that were responsible for keeping slaves under mind control. This was what they were trying to do with Allele in order to accomplish their goal of weaponizing her.

There were four soldiers standing guard; two at the door entrance and two standing on the right and left side of the chair that Allele was trapped in. There were five alchemists in the room as well.

Being the skilled fighter that he is, Zenthaus did not hesitate, charging straight for them. These guards, perhaps the best there was, still never stood a chance; they were each knocked out at almost the same time. Watching this made the alchemists very afraid, so they all proceeded to rush out in a state of terror and confusion.

Once he set Allele free from the chair, Zenthaus thought, *How close they came to changing the chemical composition of her brain. It would have been extremely difficult to reverse.*

The only thing left for them to do now is to locate Mazaya, and then they could leave this place for good. But first, Zenthaus had to figure out how to navigate his way through this enormous multilevel stone computer complex.

Taking a deep breath and closing his eyes, Zenthaus was able to locate Mazaya telepathically right away by broadcasting his thoughts. He sent her a message, letting her know to meet him in the courtyard section, where they first met each other near the exit.

What about the other slaves? he pondered. There was no need to abort the mission, but Zenthaus knew that he had to come up with a plan and fast.

Looking up, he noticed that the entire ceiling was glass, a crystal dome matrix made of compressed hydrogen, which is technology and engineering combined with artificial light responsible for projecting the simulated construct around them. And above that were five massive water tanks.

How could he even conceive the thought of breaching these water tanks, knowing how dangerous it could be?

Because it gave birth to an idea to create a flood by using these bodies of water. Zenthaus knew that when water breaks, new life begins.

Wondering if Allele could remember her training, Zenthaus discreetly asked her to concentrate and put all her focus on the dome above.

Throwing her hands out, Allele shot her photon particles at the dome, making a huge fracture in it and causing water to rush in. Out of the whole Dragon Court empire, this would be only one of many megalithic structures that they had built all throughout Pangaea.

Zenthaus thought that by flooding this building, they would be able to escape as well as disestablish this location, giving these double-minded slaves a reason to leave and eventually, when the mind-control drugs wear off, a fighting chance hopefully.

At this point there was no other choice. With the water pouring in unstoppably in such large amounts, the area was filling up quickly. This made getting to Mazaya even more imperative.

On their way through, they saw how the people were in a panic, splashing around frantically, looking for the first exit they can find out of there. It was a good thing for Zenthaus since he had no other way of making them leave

The water was waist-deep, and Zenthaus had to start swimming; but Allele was able to float, not on the water, but above it, levitating midair.

When they had seen Mazaya, she was already waiting at the entrance with a large number of slaves, and the firewall gates were still shut and locked from the inside. People were starting to drown.

Allele had to take it upon herself to do something, but in a state of shock, her conscious mind could not quite grasp the reality of what was happening.

Watching her mother and Zenthaus struggle to keep from drowning, Allele had to go within herself and reflect on her unlimited and infinite potential, reaching such a level of awareness that her hands began to glow red hot and radiant like the sun. Instinctively, she flew up to the top of the entrance wall. Using just her hand, she cut through the wall all the way down to the bottom, melting it at the same time.

A mixture of watery debris and people rushed out the other side onto the ground as if they were being symbolically reborn.

The air was fresh and new. The sky was a different kind of blue.

These slaves were raised in captivity, and never had they experienced the outside world.

"What about the Dragon Court? Will they come for us? And where will we go?" said Mazaya.

Zenthaus said, "If they come for us, we will band together, and we will fight. The Octagons are multidimensional beings that can move in or out of any realm they choose, so if they or the Dragon Court do return, we will be ready.

"As for us, we are free to do whatever we want now. These people can go their own way and start over if they want, or we can come together, form a community, and become a family.

"What do you think?" he said.

"I don't know what to think, but all I can say is that we have the highest level of respect and appreciation for you coming into our lives and saving us. I have loved you ever since," Mazaya said.

"If you let me, I will live for you and die for you," he promised.

"You don't have to be afraid. We have so much life ahead of us."

"We will figure this out. And right now, this is where I want to be—with you, and we as one."

"It is my greatest and deepest honor to share this experience with you. I am filled with much joy in this connection with you, and for that I am grateful."

"Your soul is very beautiful to me," he said.

"With you I am so much more fulfilled, and it is truly a gift to be with you."

As they all look up, watching the Dragon Court take to the sky on their airships and fly off into the distance, they shout for joy, making distinctive sounds, tones, and vibrations.

It was a cheerful moment. A feeling of peace and calmness fell upon them, knowing that they now have a way of protecting this realm and keeping it safe.

Although it may have been only the beginning of their fight for freedom, it was also the ending of doubt and uncertainty. Now began the birth of a new golden age, an age where nothing was hidden nor kept secret any longer, only revealed.

The Age of Pure Light!

ABOUT THE AUTHOR

S tefan Durham is a person of many gifts and talents—a musician, a singer-songwriter, a specialist in interior design, just to name a few. On his spare time while redefining luxury, he provides a rare and unique perspective on life in order to raise the value of those around him. A humanitarian and environmentalist, he is committed to understanding the true nature of reality. Anyone who knows him can tell that family comes first and that he is also open to new ideas, experiences, and possibilities. He is a creative force to be reckoned with.

www.ingramcontent.com/pod-product-compliance
Lightning Source LLC
Chambersburg PA
CBHW031641170726
47990CB00018B/1593